Have a Go, Sam!

Written by Leonie Bennett

Illustrated by Julie Park

ICE SKATING

Book A Lesson

Fun For All The Family

ICE HOCKEY

SPEED SKATING

2

Tilak's dad took Tilak skating.
Sam and Bobby went too.

Tilak's dad got them all some skates,
and they put them on.

'Let's go!' shouted Bobby.
'Look at me! I can go fast!'
Away he went.

'Look at me!' shouted Tilak.
'I can go backwards!'
Away he went.

'Look at me!' shouted Bobby.
'I can go on one leg!'
Away he went again.

But Sam couldn't even walk!
He watched Bobby and Tilak.

'I wish I could go fast,' he said.
'I wish I could go backwards.
I wish I could go on one leg.
How do you do it?'

'Have a go, Sam!' said Tilak.
'This is what you do.'
He went forwards ...

... and he went backwards.

He went fast ...

... and he went on one leg.

So Sam let go of Tilak's dad, and
away he went.
He landed on his bottom!

Tilak helped him up.

'Let's go and get some chips,' he said.

'Then you can have another go.'

Sam still couldn't walk, so Tilak
helped him.

'Here are your chips!' said the man.
'Don't drop them!'

But ...

'I'm sorry!' cried Sam,
'but I can't walk in my skates!'

'I can see that,' said the lady,
'and I can see why.'
'Can you?' said Sam.

'Yes,' said the lady. 'I am a
skating teacher.
I can see that your skates are too big.'

The skating teacher took Sam to
get some new skates.

'Now have a go, Sam!' she said.

She helped Sam. Bobby and
Tilak watched them.

Sam went forwards

whoosh

whoosh

... and he went backwards.

whoosh

whoosh

He went fast but ...

... he still couldn't go on one leg!